Mel Bay Presents

French Pieces for Saxophone

By J. Michael Leonard

TABLE OF CONTENTS

		SAXOPHONE	PIANO
1) MENUET AND RIGAUDON	*[MAURICE RAVEL]*	2	2
2) RIGAUDON	*[MAURICE RAVEL]*	9	4
3) RÊVERIE	*[CLAUDE DEBUSSY]*	16	6
4) UN SOIR (EVENING)	*[FLORENT SCHMITT]*	23	9
5) LE COUCOU	*[LOUIS-CLAUDE DAQUIN]*	27	10
6) APRÈS UN RÊVE	*[GABRIEL FAURÉ]*	33	12
7) ROMANZA	*[CHARLES GOUNOD]*	36	13
8) INTERMEZZO	*[GEORGE BIZET]*	38	15
9) CLAIR DE LUNE	*[CLAUDE DEBUSSY]*	41	16
10) PAVANE	*[GABRIEL FAURÉ]*	47	18
11) GYMNOPÉDIE NO. 1	*[ERIK SATIE]*	55	21
12) PAVANE POUR UNE INFANTE DÉFUNTE	*[MAURICE RAVEL]*	58	22

MENUET AND RIGAUDON
From "Le Tombeau De Couperin"

Maurice Ravel
(1875–1937)

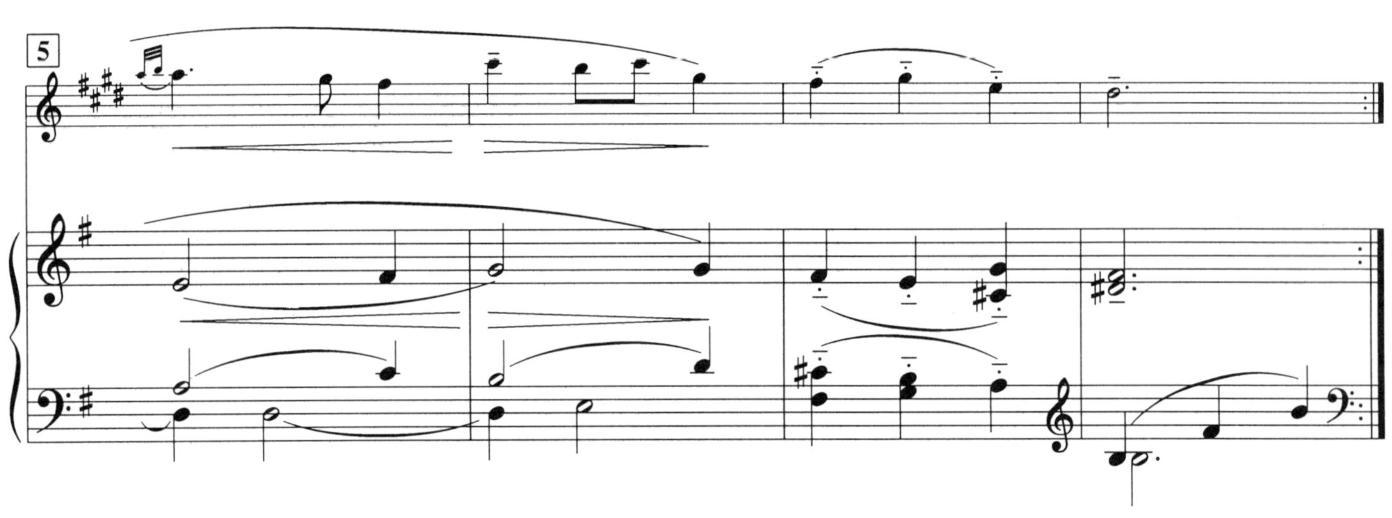

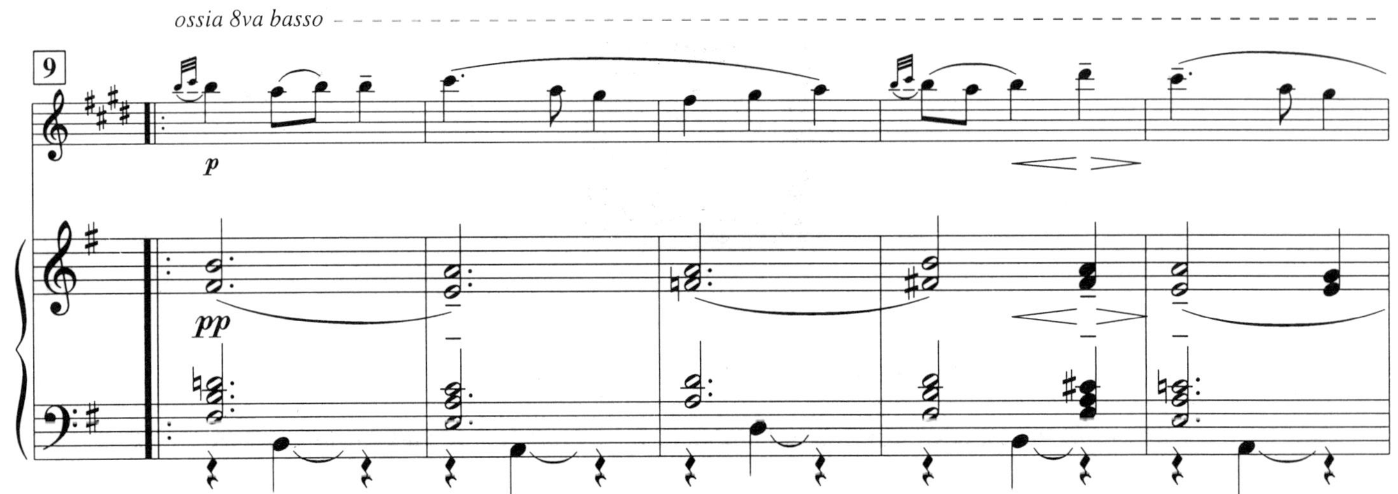

33
pp
pp
sourdine
38
43
49
p
p
3 Cordes

91
95
99
104
p expressif
pp
sourdine
p expressif
poco cresc.
pp
poco cresc.
Cordes

108
f
ff
mf
f
113
f
mf
mp
118
pp
pp
8
8
124 Ralentir Beaucoup
Trés Lent
tr
tr
sans faire vibrer

RIGAUDON
From "Le Tombeau De Couperin"

Maurice Ravel
(1875–1937)

9

29
33
Moins vif
37
p
pp
43
f
f
ff
ff

49
55
61
soutenu
soutenu
66
dim.
pp

93
Tempo I
ff
mp
ff
mp
98
ff
ff
ff
mf
mf
103
108
f
f

RÊVERIE

Claude Debussy
(1862–1918)

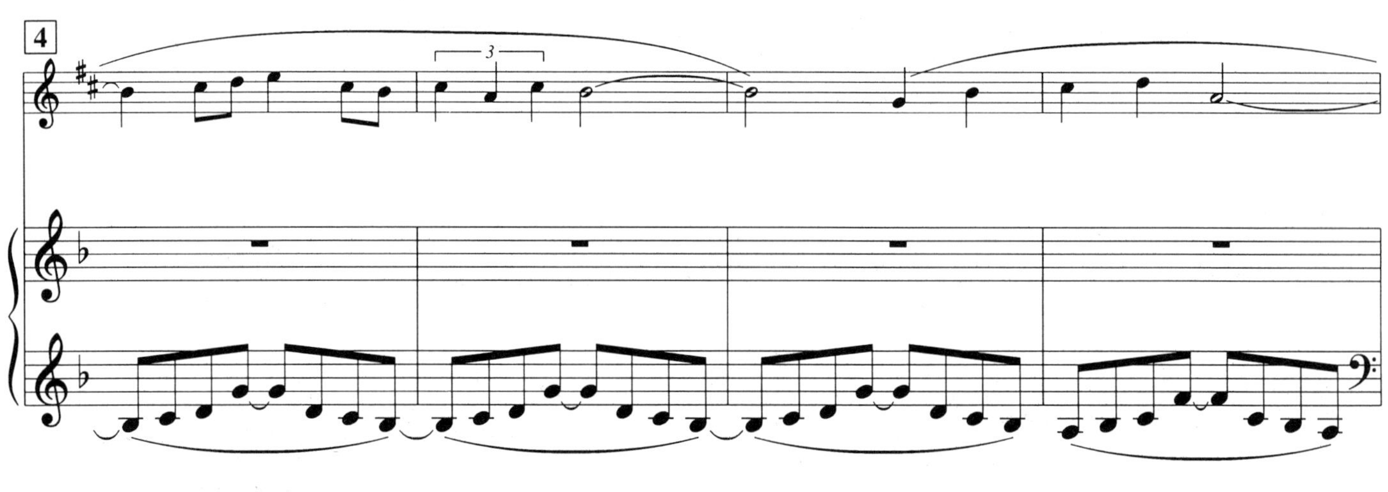

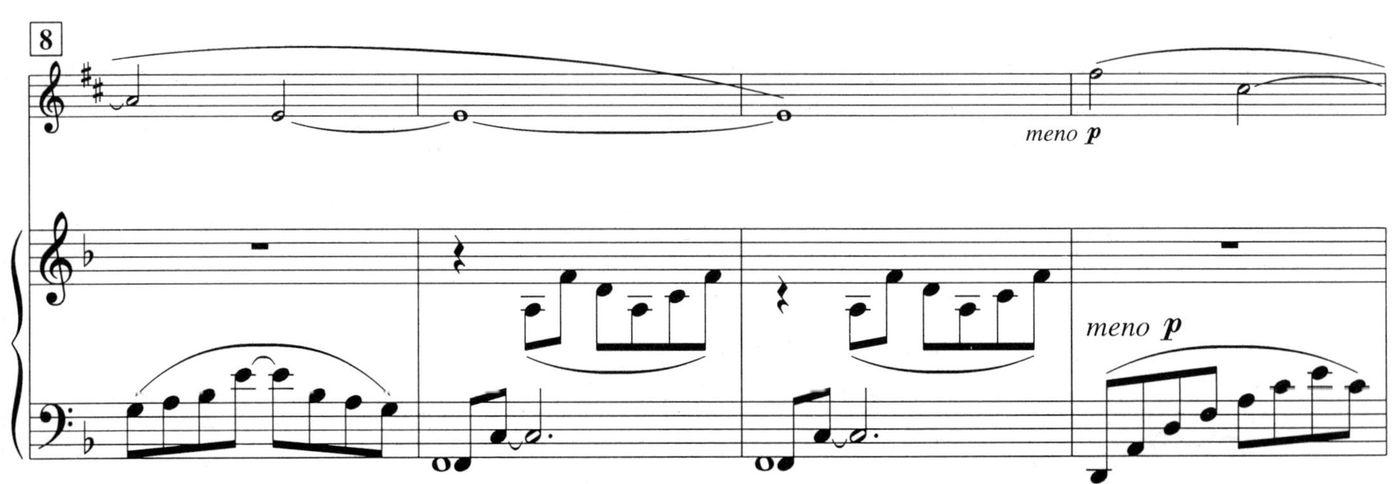

12
mf
mf
15
dim.
8va (ossia)
dim.
18
poco rit.
a tempo
p
poco rit.
pp a tempo
21
3
poco cresc.
3
poco cresc.

24
più cresc.
più cresc.
27
f
p
f
p
f
p
f
p
31
dim.
dim.
35
pp espress.

39
8va (ossia)
mf
pp
sf
43
dim.
mf
dim.
47
8va (ossia)
p rit.
p rit.
51
a tempo
p a tempo
mp
3
più p

55
mp
3
3
più p
59
p
3
pp
64
cresc.
mf
3
cresc.
mf
3
3
69
p
3
3
mp
p
più p
3

72
Tempo I
8va (ossia)
75
poco rit.
poco rit.
p
p
pp
78
82
meno p
meno p

86
p
p
p
p
90
8va (ossia)
p un poco ritenuto
p un poco ritenuto
94
3
più p
più p
98
pp
rit. e perdendosi
3
pp
rit. e perdendosi

UN SOIR (EVENING)

From "Soirs, Op. 5"

Florent Schmitt
(1870–1958)

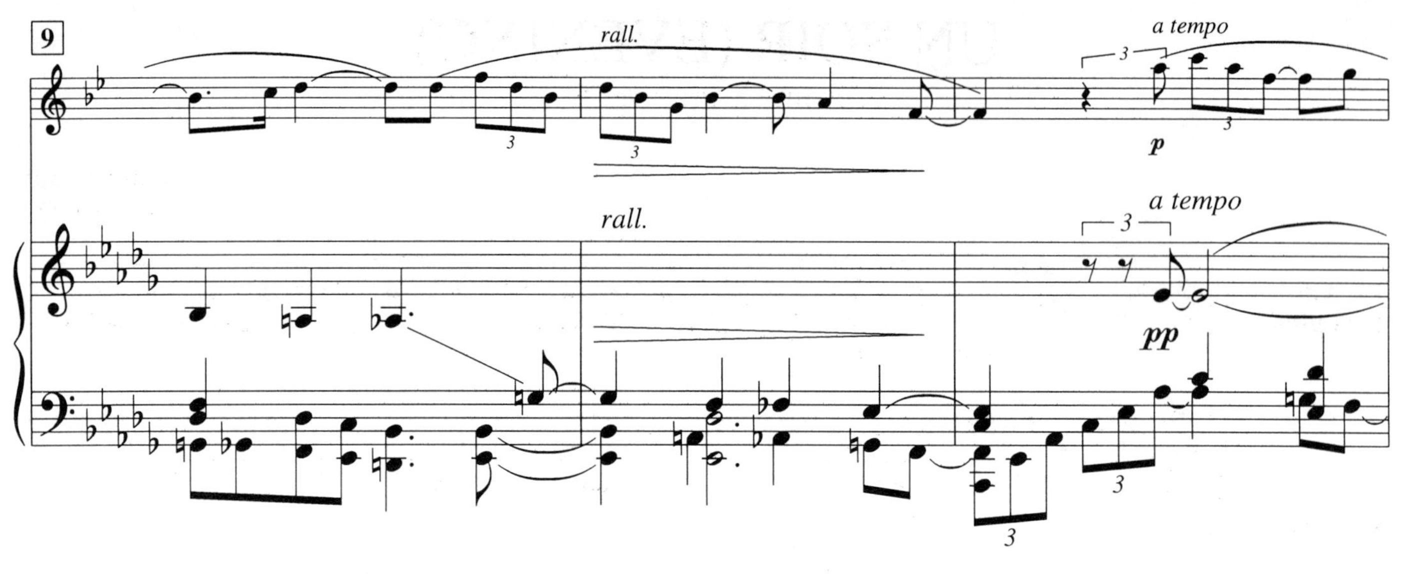

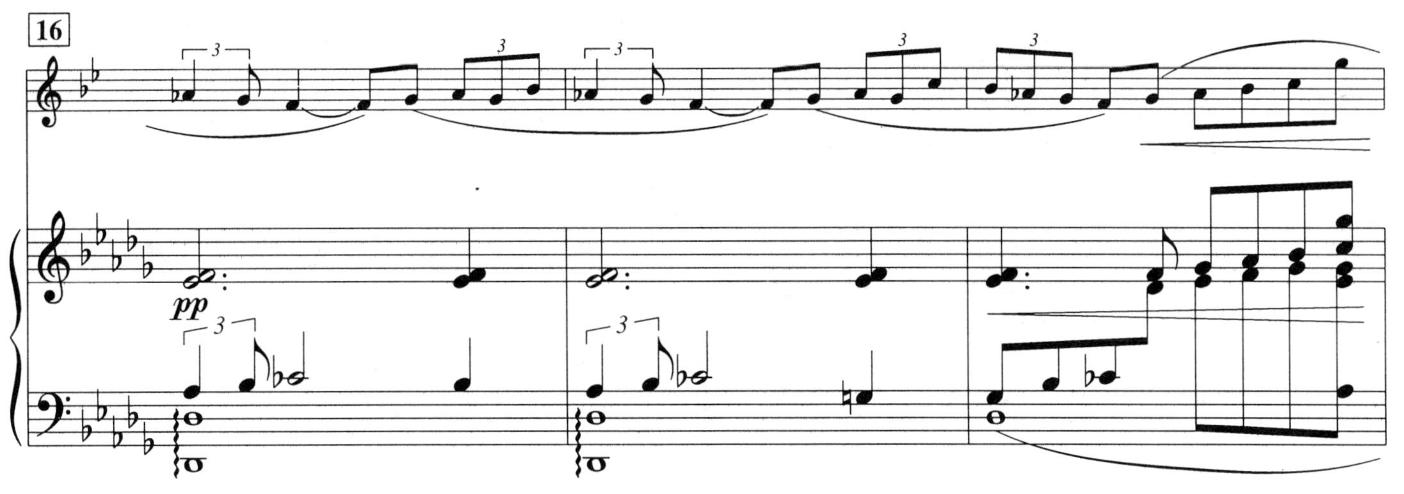

pressez
pressez

rall.
dim.
mp
rall.
dim.
p

25
a tempo
a tempo
p
pp

28
rall.
rall.
mf

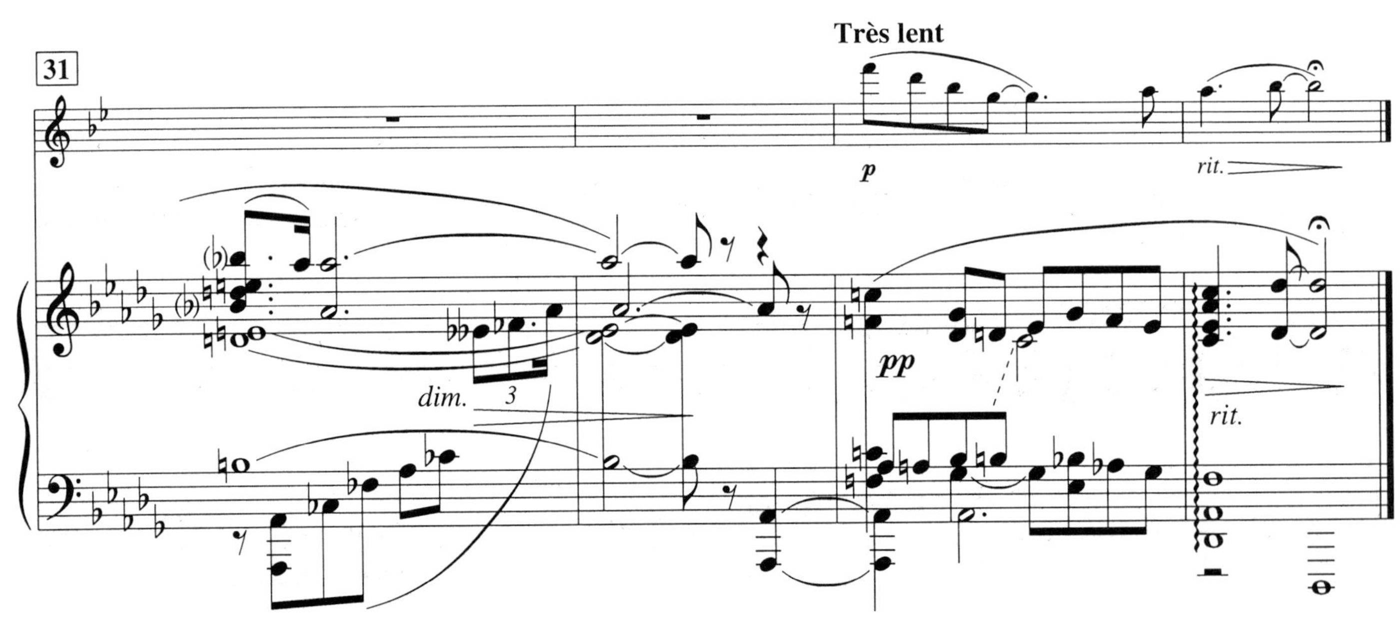

Très lent
31
p
rit.
dim.
pp
rit.

LE COUCOU

(The Cuckoo)
Rondeau

Louis–Claude Daquin
(1694–1772)

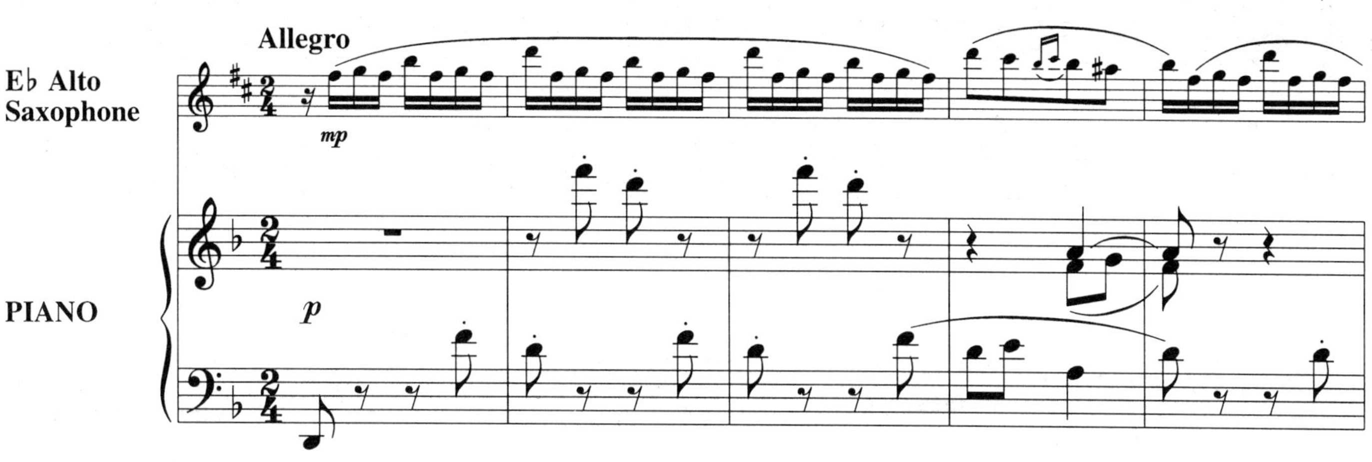

57
62
tr
p
pp
67
cresc. poco a poco
72

77
tr
mp
p
83
88
poco rit.
a tempo
poco rit.
a tempo
8
93
8
8

APRÈS UN RÊVE

(After a Dream)

Gabriel Fauré
(1845–1924)

ROMANZA

Charles Gounod
(1818–1893)

13
mf
17
mp
p
21
f
mf
25
poco rit.
poco rit.

INTERMEZZO
From L'arlésienne Suite No. 2

George Bizet
(1838–1875)

CLAIR DE LUNE
From "Suite Bergamasque"

Claude Debussy
(1862–1918)

41

Tempo rubato
pp
poco a poco cresc. et animé
poco a poco cresc. et animé

25
Un poco mosso
dim. molto
dim. molto
pp
29
p
p
32
p
p
4
4
35
cresc.
cresc.
43

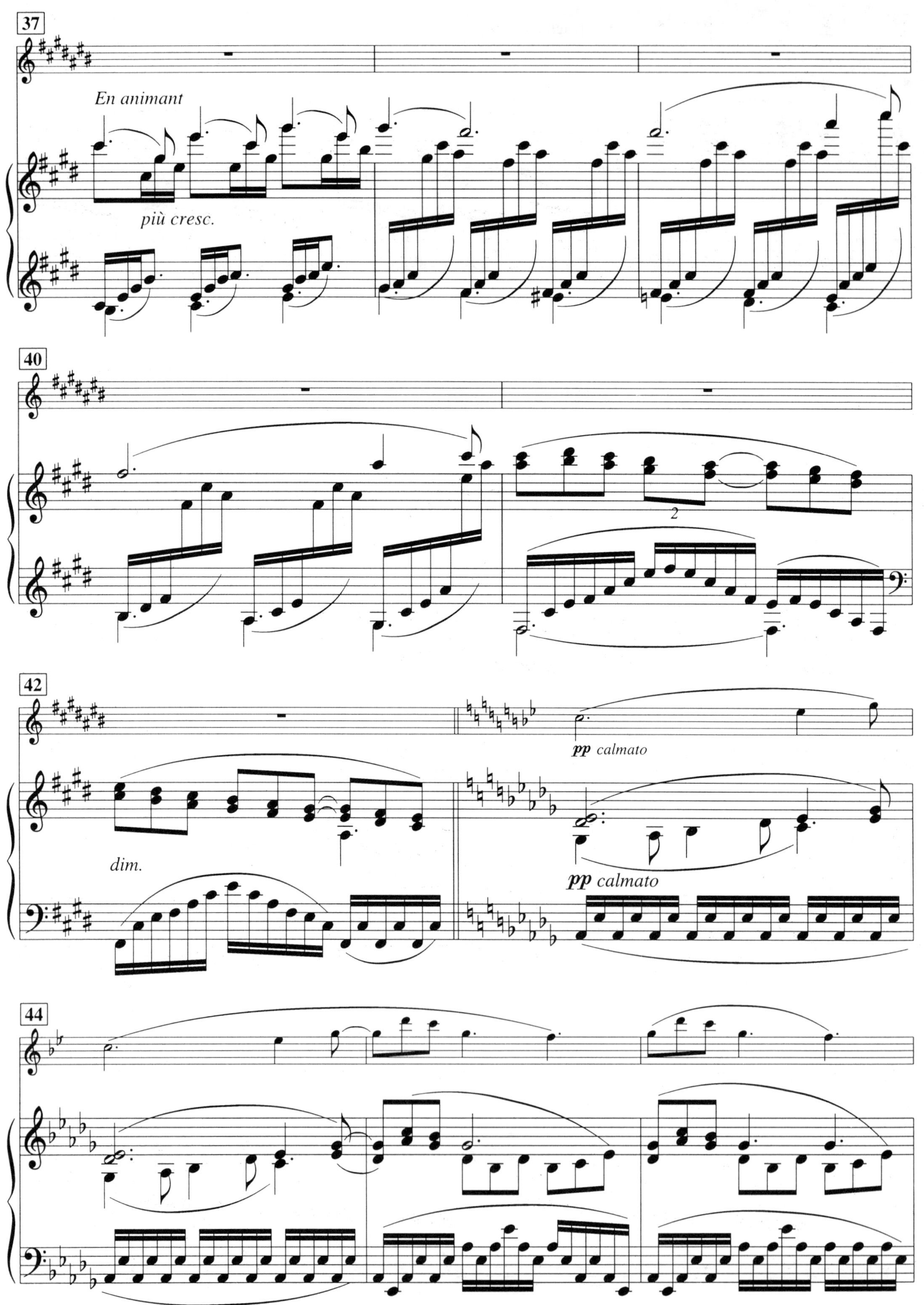

En animant
più cresc.
dim.
pp calmato
pp calmato

47
50
1° Tempo
ppp
ppp
53
2
2
2
2
56
2
45

59
pp
63
morendo jusqu'à la fin
pp
morendo jusqu'à la fin
pp
67
70

PAVANE
Op. 50

Gabriel Fauré
(1845–1924)

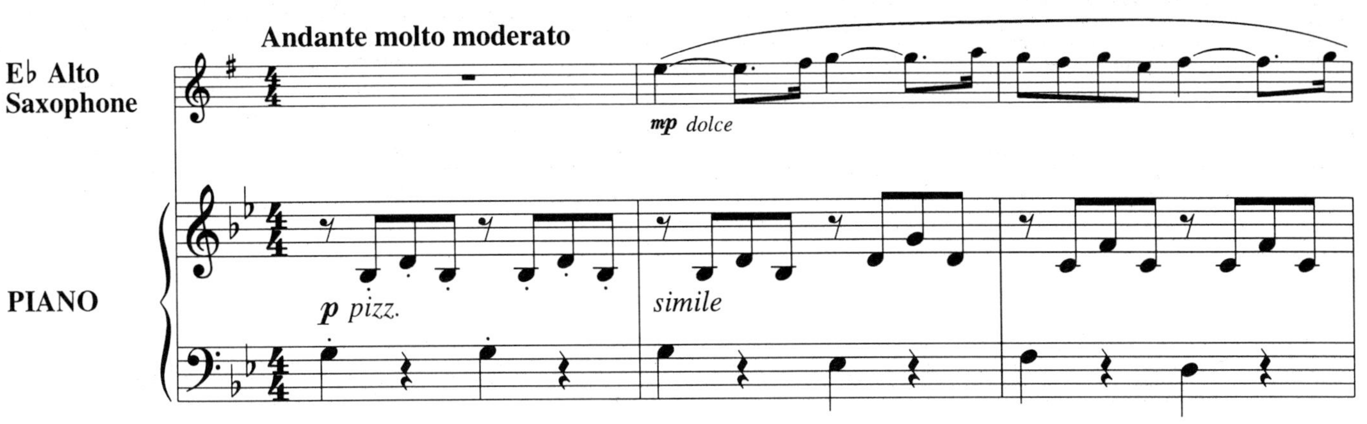

12
16
20
24
3
3
3
3
3
tr
con grazia
mp
p

80
p
pp
83
p
mf
pp
86
sfz
p
mf
pp
p
89
p espress.
3
3

GYMNOPÉDIE NO. 1

PAVANE POUR UNE INFANTE DÉFUNTE

un peu retenu
En èlargissant
1er Mouvt.
ff
f
un peu retenu
pp
p
3
Très lointain
pp
pp
m. g.
m. g.
mf très soutenu
mf très soutenu
2/4
8va (ossia)
ppp
ppp
Ped.
Ped.
Ped.
Ped.
Ped.
Ped.
2/4

22
pp
pp
25
un peu plus lent
8va (ossia)
mf
un peu plus lent
mf
f
f
28
Reprenez le mouvement
p
p
simile
Ped.
Ped.
Ped.
31
cèdez
mf
cèdez
mf

En mesure
34
rapide
p
p
un peu retenu
37
pp
Large
ff
3
p
pp un peu retenu
ff
3
subitement
1er mouvement
40
très doux et très lié
très doux et très lié
3
3
Ped.
43
p
pp
3
Ped.

46
Très grave
f
ff
sf
p
f
ff
sf
p
49
pp
3
mf
mf
52
3
3
p
6
Très grave

55
mf
sf
ff
mf
sf
ff
3
3
3
3
57
Très grave
sf
p
sf
p
p
1er Mouvement
marquez le chart
60
p
marquez le chart
p
simile
Ped.
Ped.

62
64
cédez
cédez
66
Reprenez le mouvement
pp
pp
p
69
En èlargissant beaucoup
pp
f
m.g.
m.g.
pp
f
Ped. Ped. Ped.